A **Dr. Seuss Beginner Fun Book**™

I CAN ADD UPSIDE DOWN!

LEARN ABOUT EASY ADDITION

Adapted by Linda Hayward
and Cathy Goldsmith
from the works of

Dr. Seuss

Random House 🏠 New York

TM & © 1995 by Dr. Seuss Enterprises, L.P. All rights reserved under International and Pan-American Copyright Conventions. Published in the United States by Random House, Inc., New York, and simultaneously in Canada by Random House of Canada Limited, Toronto. ISBN 0-679-86754-6
Manufactured in the United States of America   10 9 8 7 6 5 4 3 2

First of all

there are some things
you should know.

I crossed out one.

        2

I circled one.

①   2

I underlined one.

<u>1</u>   2

I wrote the answer.

$$1 + 1 = \boxed{2}$$

And next a word about sets.

You can have sets of trees...

or bees...

or knees.

But what is true about all these sets?

All of <u>these</u> are sets of 3.

1 + 1 = 2

How many yellow Wosets in closets? 2

How many purple Wosets in closets? 1

How many Wosets in closets in all? 2

Cross out the set of 1.

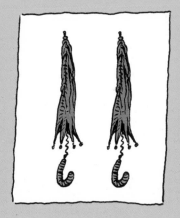 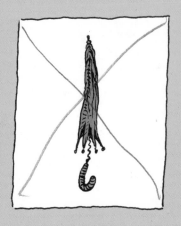 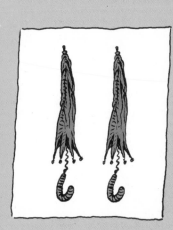

2 + 1 = 3

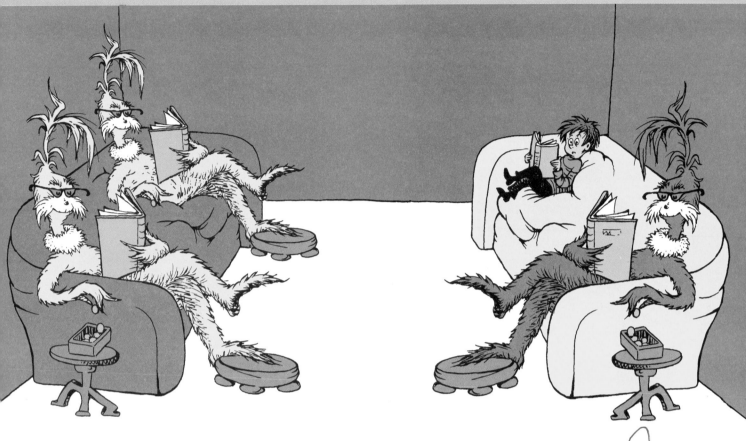

How many yellow Bofas on sofas?

How many purple Bofas on sofas?

How many Bofas on sofas in all?

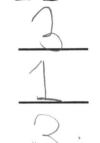

Circle the set of 3.

 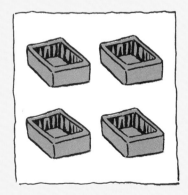 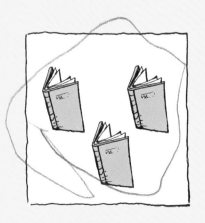

$1 + 0 = 1$

How many wide-awake Zelves on shelves? 1

How many fast-asleep Zelves on shelves? 0

How many Zelves on shelves in all? 1

Circle the set of 0.

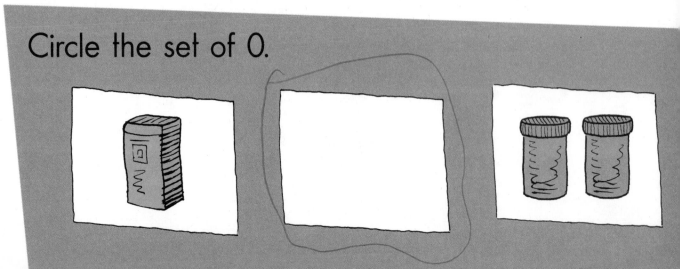

1 + 3 = 4

How many tall Zowers in showers? ___1___

How many small Zowers in showers? ___3___

How many Zowers in showers in all? ___4___

Cross out the set of 2.

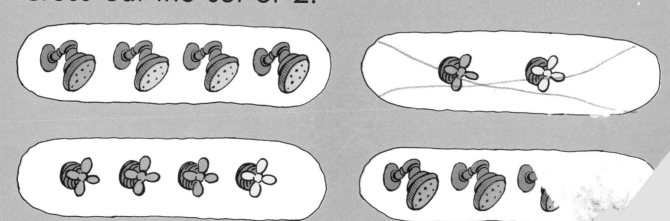

0 + 0 = 0

How many Zalls fall in the hall? _____

How many Zalls playing ball in the hall? _____

How many Zalls in the hall in all? _____

Cross out the set of 1.

I can add in red.

0 + 0 = **0**

2 + 1 = **3**

2 + 0 = **2**

I can add in blue.

1 + 1 = **2**

1 + 2 = **3**

1 + 3 = **4**

I can add in pickle color too.

$$\begin{array}{r} 1 \\ +\ 1 \\ \hline \mathbf{2} \end{array} \qquad \begin{array}{r} 2 \\ +\ 1 \\ \hline \mathbf{3} \end{array} \qquad \begin{array}{r} 1 \\ +\ 2 \\ \hline \mathbf{3} \end{array} \qquad \begin{array}{r} 3 \\ +\ 1 \\ \hline \mathbf{4} \end{array}$$

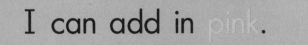

I can add in pink.

$0 + 0 = 0$

$1 + 0 = 1$

$2 + 0 = 2$

And in purple and brown.

$3 + 0 = 3$

$0 + 3 = 3$

I can add
in a circle...

$1 + 1 = 2$

$1 + 2 = 3$

$2 + 1 = 3$

and upside down!

How many yellow Findows in windows? $\underline{1}$

How many orange Findows in windows? $\underline{1}$

How many blue Findows in windows? $\underline{1}$

How many pink Findows in windows? $\underline{1}$

How many Findows in windows in all? $\underline{4}$

Underline the set of 4.

2 + 2 = 4

How many yellow Ninks in sinks? ___2___

How many purple Ninks in sinks? ___2___

How many Ninks in sinks in all? ___4___

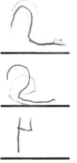

Cross out the set of 3.

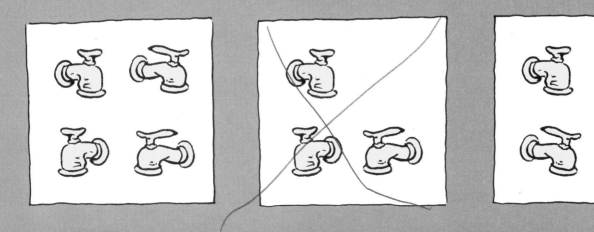

4 + 1 = 5

How many Yeps on steps
with yellow posies on toesies? _____
How many Yeps on steps
with pink posies on toesies? _____
How many Yeps on steps in all? _____

In each set,
color 4 posies yellow
and 1 posy pink.

 **+** Find the sticker that goes here. **=**

Find the sticker that goes here. **+**  **=**

 **+** Find the sticker that goes here. **=**

 **+** Find the sticker that goes here. **=**

Find the sticker that goes here. **+**  **=**

 **+** Find the sticker that goes here. **=**

I can add cats.
I can add roses.
I can add owls.
I can add noses.

How many big cats?

How many little cats?

How many cats in all?

How many pink roses?

How many yellow roses?

How many roses in all?

How many brown owls?

How many gray owls?

How many owls in all?

How many people noses?

How many cat noses?

How many noses in all?

$$2 + 3 = 5$$

How many orange Zamps in lamps? ____

How many purple Zamps in lamps? ____

How many Zamps in lamps in all? ____

In each set, color 2 lampshades blue
and 3 lampshades green.

5 + 1 = 6

How many yellow Zables on tables? ____

How many green Zables on tables? ____

How many Zables on tables in all? ____

Circle the sets of 6.

Draw a frankfurter on every fork.

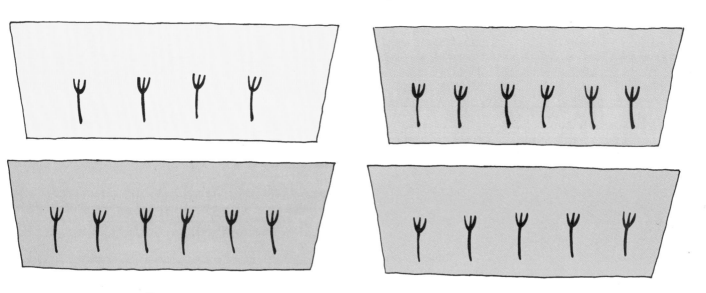

 **+**  **=**

 **+** Find the sticker that goes here. **=**

 **+** Find the sticker that goes here. **=**

Find the sticker that goes here. **+**  **=**

1 + 1 = ☐

2 + 1 = ☐

3 + 1 = ☐

4 + 1 = ☐

5 + 1 = ☐

1 + 2 = ☐

2 + 2 = ☐

3 + 2 = ☐

1 + 1 + 1 = ☐

2 + 1 + 1 = ☐

3 + 1 + 1 = ☐

4 + 1 + 1 = ☐

I can add anchors.
I can add ants.
I can add hats
and crocodile pants.

How many blue anchors?

How many green anchors?

How many anchors in all?

How many red ants?

How many black ants?

How many ants in all?

How many striped hats?

How many plain hats?

How many hats in all?

How many yellow crocodile pants?

How many purple crocodile pants?

How many crocodile pants in all?

3 + 3 = 6

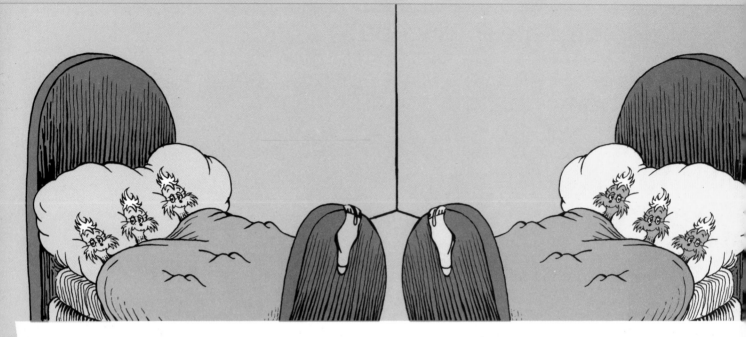

How many yellow Zillows on pillows? _____

How many pink Zillows on pillows? _____

How many Zillows on pillows in all? _____

Circle the sets of 6.

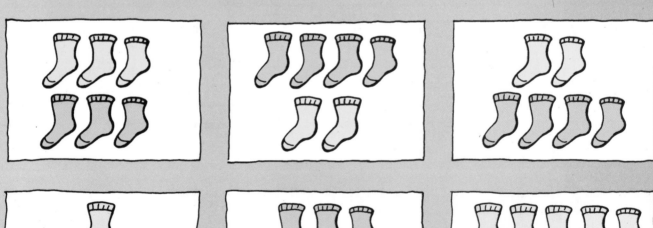

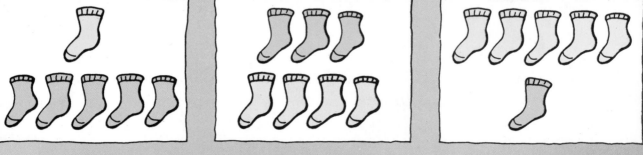

How many blue anchors? □

How many green anchors? □

How many anchors in all? □

How many red ants? □

How many black ants? □

How many ants in all? □

How many striped hats? □

How many plain hats? □

How many hats in all? □

How many yellow crocodile pants? □

How many purple crocodile pants? □

How many crocodile pants in all? □

3 + 3 = 6

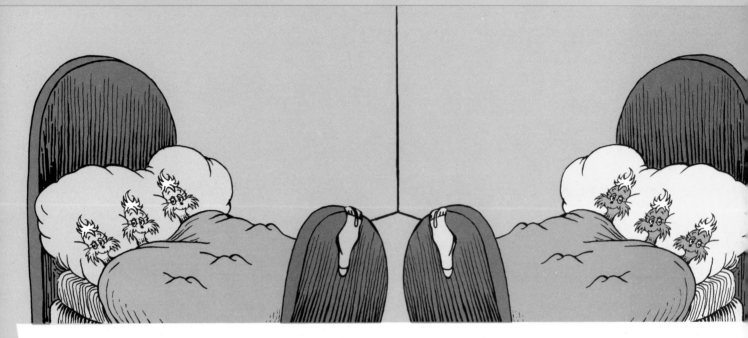

How many yellow Zillows on pillows? _____

How many pink Zillows on pillows? _____

How many Zillows on pillows in all? _____

Circle the sets of 6.

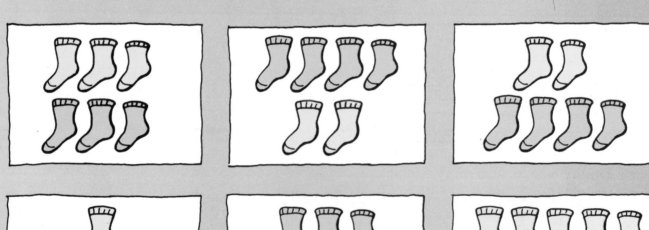

A BIT OF FUN!

MUCHLY MUCH MORE FUN!

GREAT DAY FOR FUN!

6 + 1 = 7

How many Zlocks beside blue clocks?   ____

How many Zlocks beside green clocks?   ____

How many Zlocks beside clocks in all?   ____

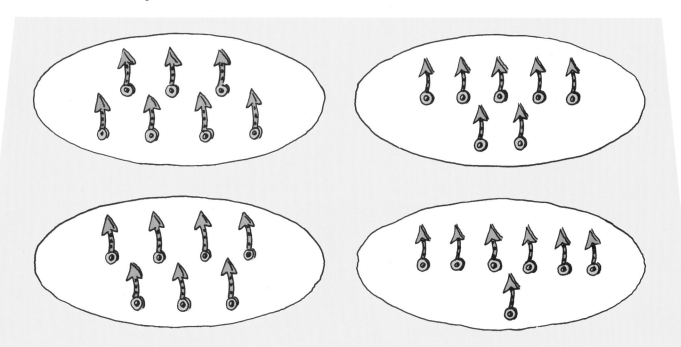

All of these are sets of ____.

Write the number.

7 + 1 = 8

How many pink Waskets in blue baskets? _____

How many blue Waskets in pink baskets? _____

How many Waskets in baskets in all? _____

In each set, color 7 scraps of paper yellow
and 1 scrap of paper green.

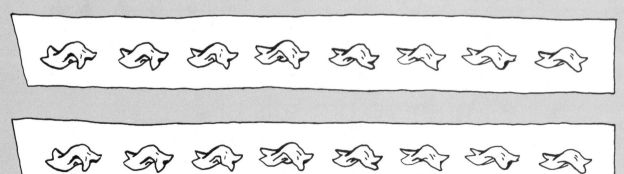

8 + 1 = 9

How many friendly Yottles in bottles? _____

How many UN-friendly Yottles in bottles? _____

How many Yottles in bottles in all? _____

Underline the sets of 9.

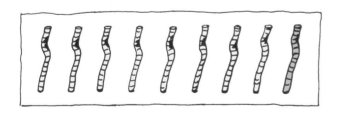

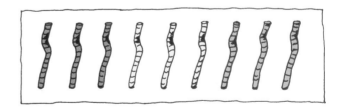

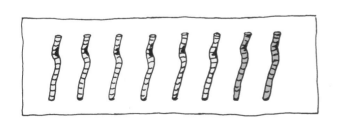

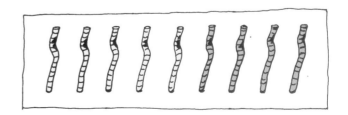

9 + 1 = 10

How many blue Nupboards in cupboards? _____

How many pink Nupboards in cupboards? _____

How many Nupboards in cupboards in all? _____

In each set, color 9 cups blue and 1 cup pink.

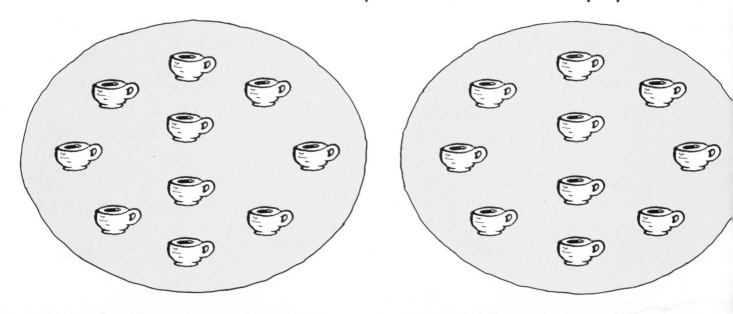

Find the sticker that goes here.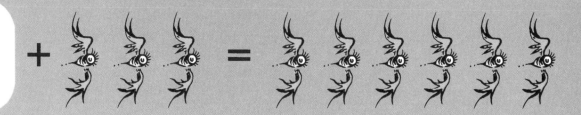

 + Find the sticker that goes here. =

 + Find the sticker that goes here. =

 + Find the sticker that goes here. =

Find the sticker that goes here. +

 + Find the sticker that goes here. =

I can add going up.
I can add going down.
I can add in my car
on the way into town.

1 + 2 + 3 + 4 = 10

How many Yots in yellow pots? _____

How many Yots in purple pots? _____

How many Yots in green pots? _____

How many Yots in blue pots? _____

How many Yots in pots in all? _____

I can add here
and all over town.
I can add up
and upside down!

(signed) ....